Dopie Dope
Goes to the Fair

Poetry for Children

by Joe Larke
Illustrated by Karol Larke

FIRST EDITION

To order additional copies write to:
GRIN-A-BIT COMPANY
P.O. BOX 235
ROCKWALL, TEXAS 75087

Published by GRIN-A-BIT CO., INC.
Rockwall, Texas
Printed by Taylor Publishing Company, Dallas, Texas
Helen Lance, Publication Consultant

ISBN 0-9620112-7-4

PREFACE

"Dopie Dope" originated in our first book, *The Bullfrog and the Grasshopper and Other Tails.* It is a short four-line poem about a guy who doesn't use soap when he bathes. He has become extremely popular with children. Dopie Dope also appears in our second book, *Can't Reach the Itch,* and our third book, *Two Pigs in Wigs.* Dopie's popularity has demanded an entire "Dopie Dope" poetry book be made available to all of his fans. So . . . here it is.

One morning early "Dopie Dope"
Was knocking on our door,
The moment we saw who it was
We both hit the floor.

We knew what Dopie wanted
He told us yesterday,
He wants to take us to the fair
And said he'd pay our way.

Last night we thought it over
But Dopie doesn't know,
Because he doesn't bathe in soap
We don't want to go.

He peeked in our front window
Wondering what to do,
He wrote and left a message
And signed it,"youknowwho!"

It said, "I left here early,"
Then as he skipped away,
He sang, "I'm going to the fair
Ha ha, Ho ho, Hooray."

Dopie got excited
He didn't want to wait.
By the time he got there
He ran right through the gate.

TICKETS

9

The ticket taker shouted
And called ol' Dopie, "Bub."
"Bring that ticket back to me
I've gotta have the stub."

Dopie didn't know
They wanted the ticket back.
He knew he had to have one
And was headed for a snack.

The ticket taker took too long
To tear it down the middle.
Dopie said, "You're wasting time;
I didn't come to piddle."

Dopie bought some popcorn,
Ice cream and a coke.
He brought a bunch of money
And will spend it 'til he's broke.

Dopie loves to eat
Especially fair "junk" stuff.
No matter how much Dopie eats
He never gets enough.

So he got himself a hot dog,
Squeezed mustard through a spout.
He got so much — when he bit down
The wienee shot right out!

13

As usual Dopie smells bad,
But now has stained his shirt.
With chili from his hot dog
And a splattered mustard spurt.

He's stuffed his hungry stomach;
He's ready for a ride.
Which one will he make his first?
Dopie can't decide.

He walks up to the Ferris
wheel,
But when he sees how high,
It is from bottom to the top
It's NO, NO! — and BYE, BYE!

As Dopie starts to walk
He can't pick up his feet.
Two big wads of bubble gum
Have glued him to concrete.

He pulls and pulls and pulls
He finally gets unstuck.
The gum gets wrapped around him
And Dopie says, "Oh, yuk!"

He's got gum in his popcorn
Also on his pants.
He jumps and twists and kicks
Like ants are in his pants.

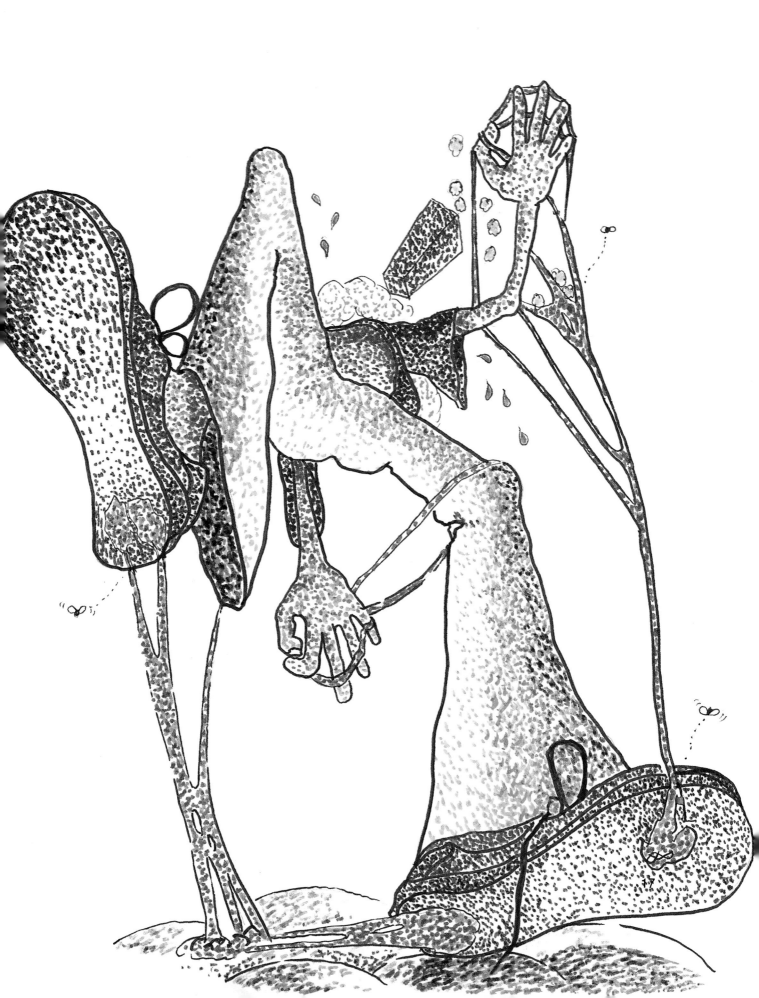

Everybody's thinking,
"Could this guy be sick?
Or is he working for the fair
Doing a stupid trick!"

He finally got untangled,
But now is soaking wet.
With all that jumping and kicking
He worked up quite a sweat.

Dopie's smelling awful.
The odor wrinkles your nose.
Getting close to Dopie
Gets "stink" all in your clothes.

Although he is exhausted,
He shouts, "I'm ready to go.
I wanna do some chunkin'
Where do I go to throw?"

The crowd all pointed that way
And that way Dopie went.
Until he found a monkey
In a dunking tent.

It stood above the water
Dressed like Dopie Dope.
You could tell by the stink on the monkey
HE doesn't wash in soap.

The monkey wore a cap
Like Dopie's but had no "D."
The cap was really too large
The monkey could barely see.

Ol' Dopie's good at chunkin'
He dunked the monkey quick.
But what ol' Dopie didn't know
The "monkey" had a trick.

He shot up from the water
Like a rocket into space.
His mouth was full of water
He spewed in Dopie's face.

Dopie wiped the water
With a hankey from the crowd.
"Cheers" were for the monkey
That made the crowd right proud.

Dopie said, "Oh, pfttt!
There's better places to be.
This monkey ain't the only thing
I came today to see."

Next he stood in line
To ride the bumper cars.
His car got hit so many times
All he saw was stars.

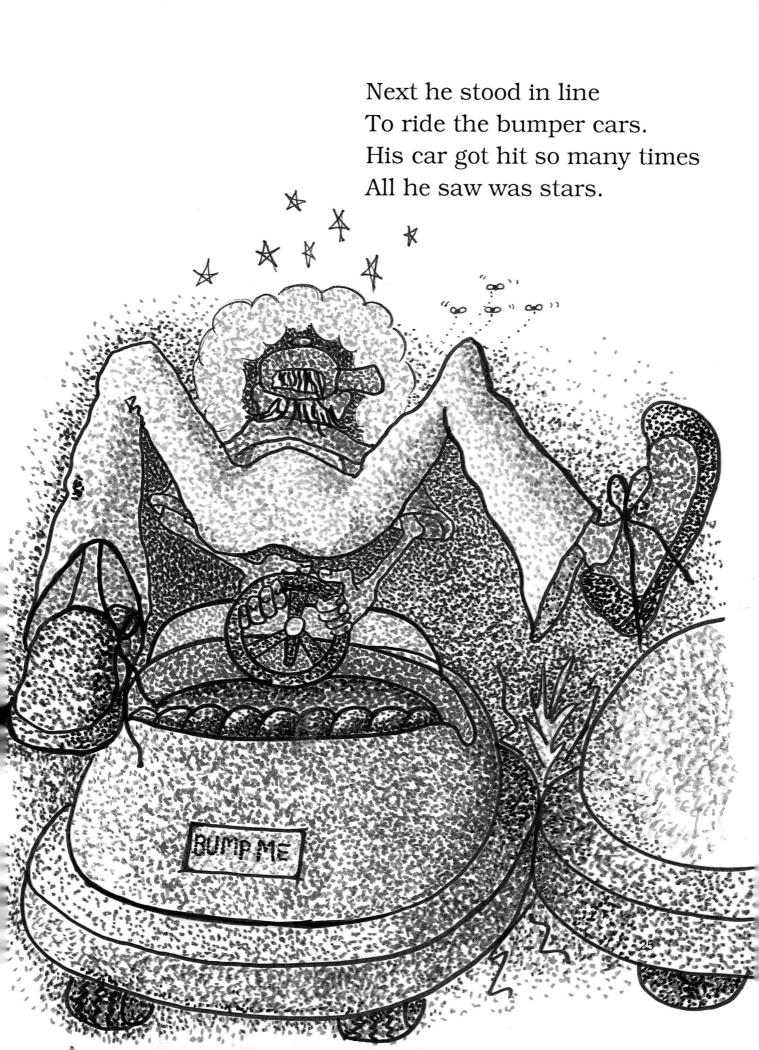

BUMP ME

Then he found a shootin' booth
Installed with a water gun.
The trick was to hit each target
Like the other shooters had done.

Dopie pulled the trigger
Then peeked where the water went.
He thought he hit the target
But splattered the back of the tent.

It made ol' Dopie angry
He grabbed another gun.
There were 57 targets
Dopie didn't hit a one.

Again he said, "Oh, pfttt!
I can't even shoot.
Everything I've tried
Ain't been worth a hoot."

He jogged down to the "bullet"
Climbed in for a ride.
He didn't see the "cutie"
Sitting by his side.

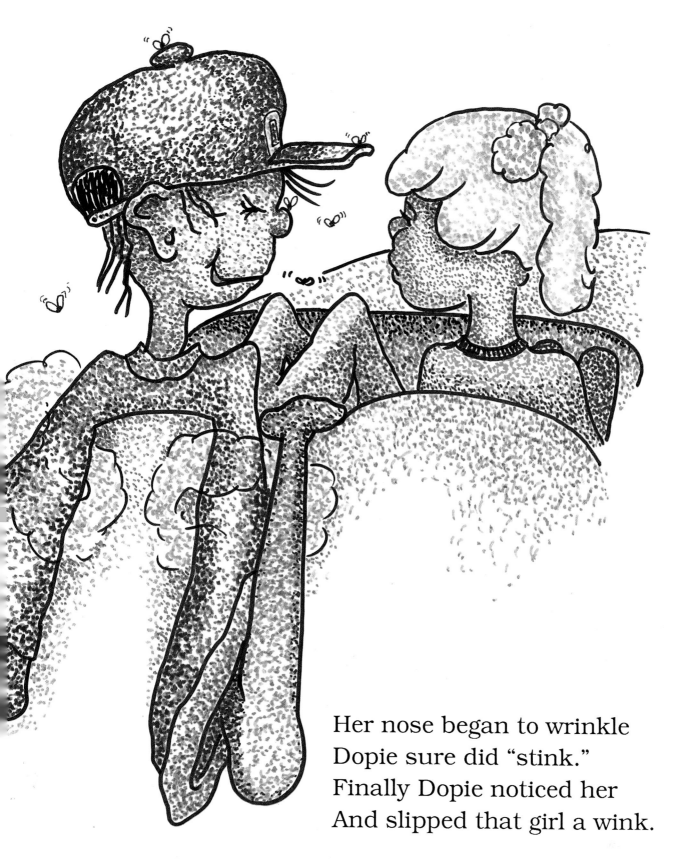

Her nose began to wrinkle
Dopie sure did "stink."
Finally Dopie noticed her
And slipped that girl a wink.

He never had a chance
To tell the "cutie" hello,
The bullet took off quickly
And boy did that thing go!

Dopie's legs were hanging out
As the bullet spun 'round and 'round.
Dopie was shoutin' and screamin',
"Get me to the ground!"

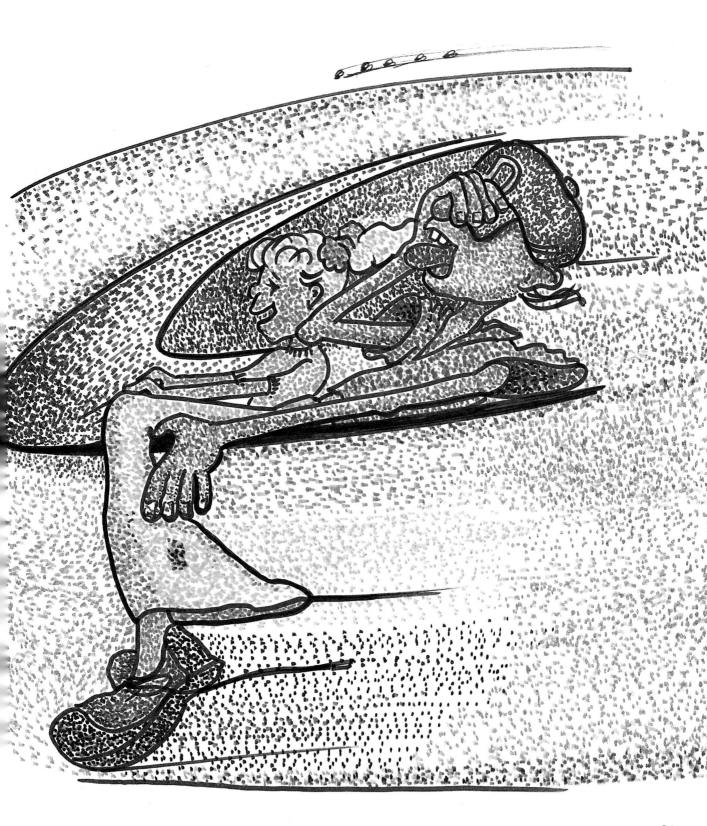

Faster and faster it circled.
Dopie began to shout,
"Hey man, I don't want to ride this ride
Please just get me OUT!"

The "cutie" riding by him
Was smiling with delight.
You KNOW what she was thinking . . .
"This just serves him right."

Finally, the ride was over,
You know what Dopie said?
"Whoever rides this crazy ride
Has nuthin' for a head."

Dopie was dizzy and wobbling,
He walked into a tree,
He thought is was somebody
And said to the tree, "Scuse me."

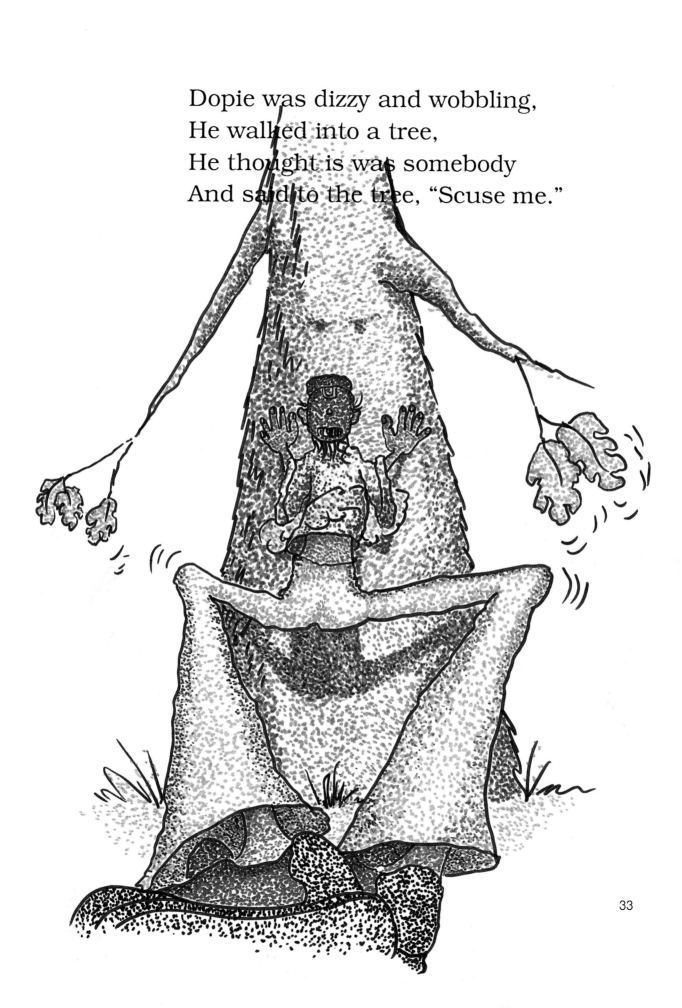

He wanted cotton candy.
Ten cents got him some.
He looked at it and wondered,
"Where does this come from?"

He found that cotton sticky.
Did he make a mess?
With cotton on his nose and cap
You know the answer's "YES."

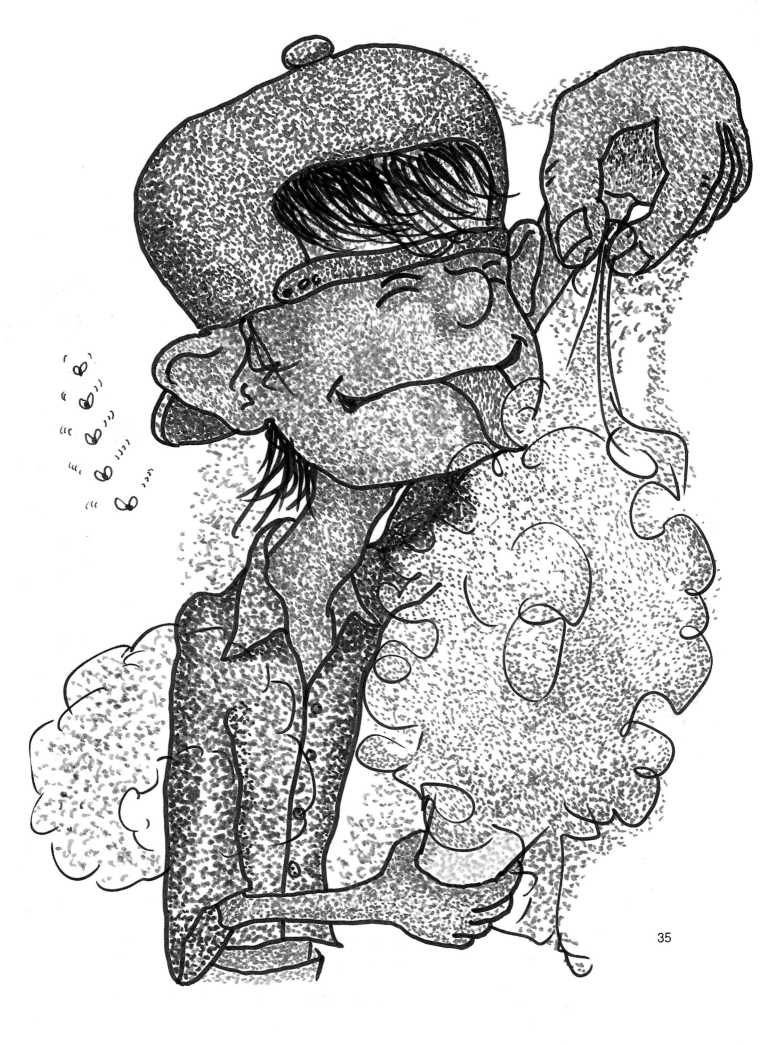

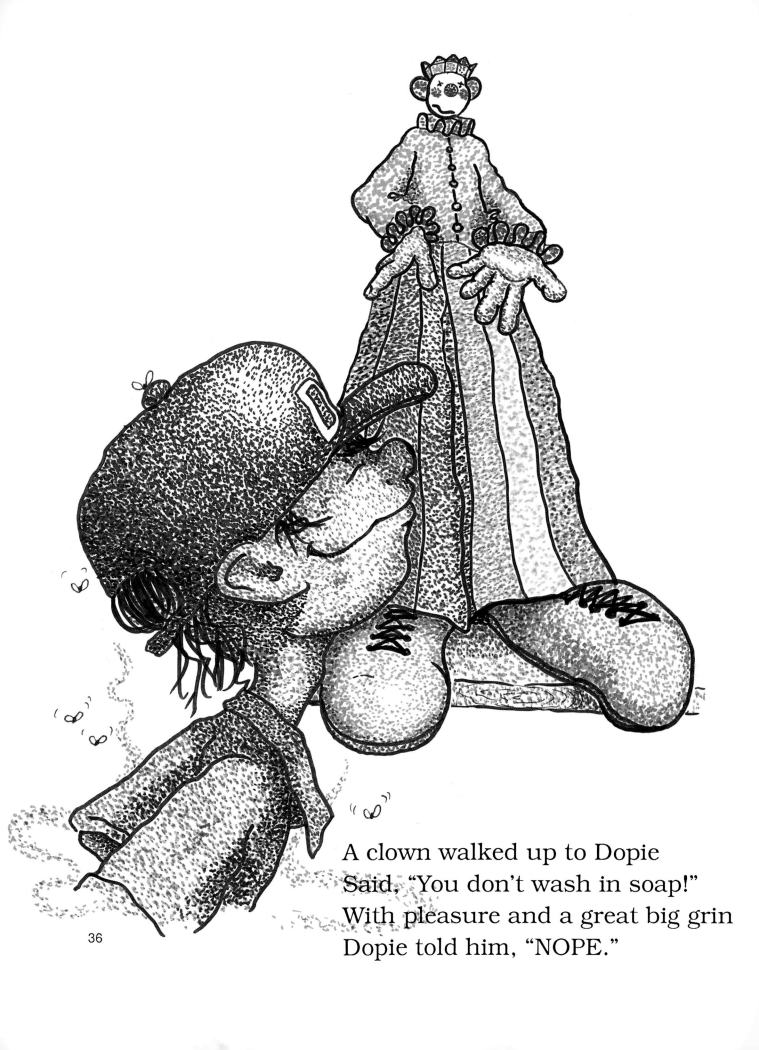

A clown walked up to Dopie
Said, "You don't wash in soap!"
With pleasure and a great big grin
Dopie told him, "NOPE."

36

About that time a whistle blew
For time to leave the park.
Every day the fair is closed
When daylight turns to dark.

The crowd was squeezed together
While going out the gate.
The opening was so narrow
Many had to wait.

The stink on Dopie drifted
To everybody there.
Many couldn't stand it
It floated everywhere.

Someone shouted, "Awful!
I wonder who is he?"
Someone else said, "I don't know,
But Oh my gosh, PEW E!!!"

Later we heard Dopie Dope
Knocking on our door.
The moment we saw who it was
We both hit the floor!

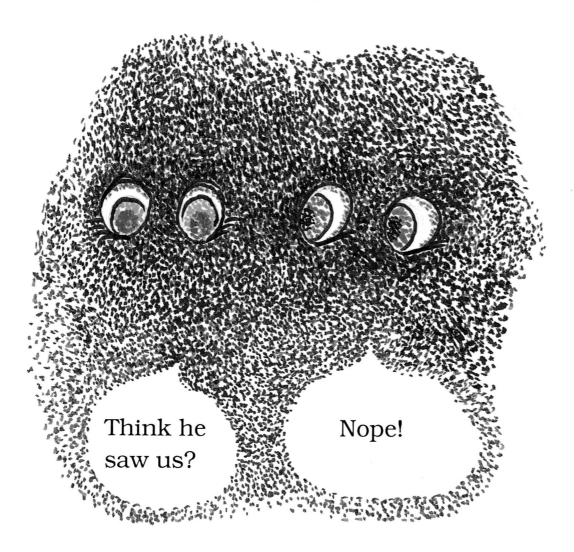